FRED BEAR and FRIENDS

AT THE
Doctor

By Melanie Joyce

WEEKLY READER®
PUBLISHING

Please visit our web site at www.garethstevens.com
For a free catalog describing our list of high-quality books,
call 1-800-542-2595 (USA) or 1-800-387-3178 (Canada).
Our fax: 1-877-542-2596

Library of Congress Cataloging-in-Publication Data

Joyce, Melanie.
    At the doctor / Melanie Joyce. — North American ed.
       p. cm. — (Fred Bear and friends)
       Summary: Fred takes Betty to a doctor because she has a
    stomach ache. Includes facts about eating right and staying fit.
       ISBN-13: 978-0-8368-8969-7 (lib. bdg.)
       ISBN-10: 0-8368-8969-X (lib. bdg.)
       ISBN-13: 978-0-8368-8976-5 (softcover)
       ISBN-10: 0-8368-8976-2 (softcover)
       [1. Medical care — Fiction. 2. Teddy bears — Fiction.
    3. Toys—Fiction.] I. Title.
    PZ7.J8283 Ate   2008
    [E]—dc22   2007031341

This North American edition first published in 2008 by
Weekly Reader® Books
An Imprint of Gareth Stevens Publishing
1 Reader's Digest Road
Pleasantville, NY 10570-7000 USA

Gareth Stevens Senior Managing Editor: Lisa M. Guidone
Gareth Stevens Creative Director: Lisa Donovan
Gareth Stevens Art Director: Alex Davis
Gareth Stevens Associate Editor: Amanda Hudson

Photo credits (t=top, b=bottom, c=center, l=left,
r=right, bg=background)
All photography by Colin Beer of JL Allwork
Photography except for Shutterstock: 22b x 6, 24.

Every effort has been made to trace the copyright
holders for the photos used in this book, and the
publisher apologizes in advance for any
unintentional omissions. We would be pleased to
insert the appropriate acknowledgements in any
subsequent edition of this publication.

Printed in the United States of America

1 2 3 4 5 6 7 8 9 10 09 08 07

Meet Fred Bear and Friends

Also starring...

Arthur

Fred

Dolly

4

Betty, Fred, Jess, and Arthur are eating breakfast. Betty does not feel well.
"My stomach hurts," she groans.

5

Fred takes Betty to
see the doctor.

6

They have to wait their turn.
Fred and Betty sit in the waiting room.

7

"Look!" says Betty.
"Dolly is here."

She has come to
see a doctor, too.
She has a sore
throat.

Soon a nurse
calls Betty's name.

Fred goes
with Betty to
see the doctor.

9

Fred and Betty
go into the
doctor's office.

Betty lies down
on a table.
Doctor Walsh
comes in a few
minutes later.

"Hello, Betty,"
says Doctor Walsh.
"How can I
help you?"

"My stomach hurts,"
says Betty.

Doctor Walsh
presses gently on
Betty's stomach.

Doctor Walsh takes
Betty's temperature.

She also listens to Betty's heartbeat.

Thump, thump.

"You will be okay," says
Doctor Walsh. "Medicine will
make you feel better.
You will need to take
some in the morning and
some at night."

Doctor Walsh tells Betty
to stay in bed for the day.
She also tells her to drink
lots of water.

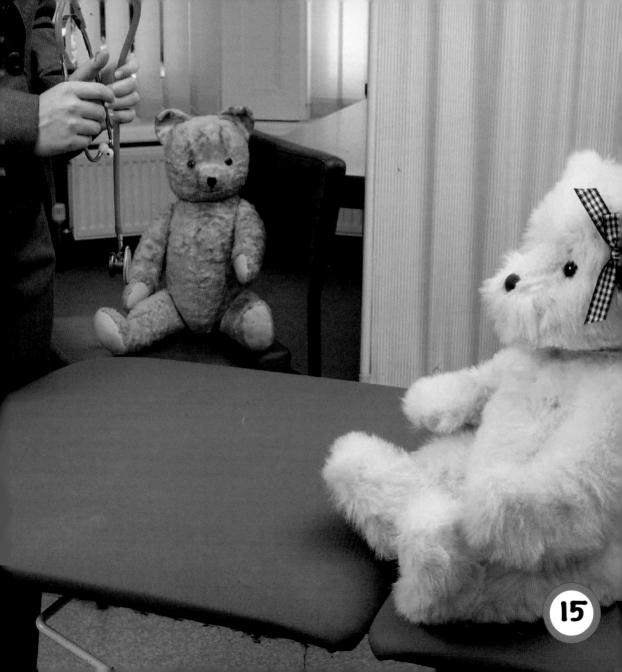

Doctor Walsh writes a special note for Betty's medicine.

The note tells the pharmacist what kind of medicine Betty needs.

Fred and Betty
say good-bye to
Doctor Walsh.

Betty goes to
the drugstore.
Dolly is there, too.
Betty and Dolly give
their special notes to
the pharmacist.

Betty gets her
medicine and a
special spoon.

19

At home, Betty
goes to bed.
She takes her medicine.
Her stomach soon
feels better.

Betty's friends
come to visit.

"Surprise!"

says Jess. "We
have a present for
you. It is a pretend
doctor's kit."

Now Betty can be
just like Doctor Walsh!

Stay Healthy

Look at the pyramid. It shows what kinds of food keep you healthy. It also show how much to eat.

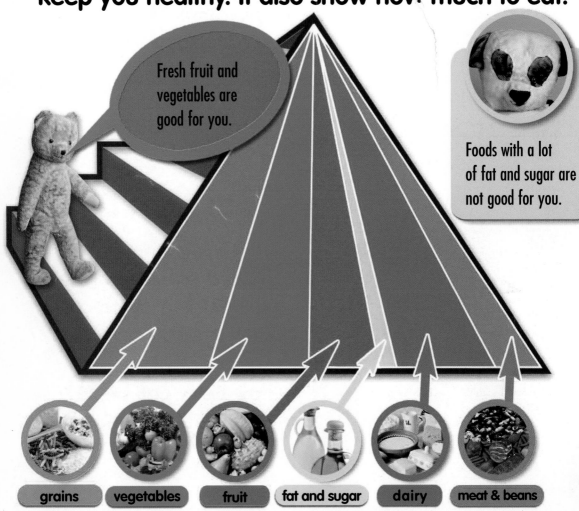

Fresh fruit and vegetables are good for you.

Foods with a lot of fat and sugar are not good for you.

grains | vegetables | fruit | fat and sugar | dairy | meat & beans

Grains such as bread and pasta are healthy. You may eat lots of these foods.

Milk, yogurt, and cheese are part of the dairy group. They help build healthy teeth and bones.

Foods such as meat, beans, fish, and chicken help build strong muscles.

Exercise!

Fred and his friends exercise every day. Here are some games they play. What is your favorite game?

Betty loves to play ball.

Dolly plays hopscotch at school.

23

Use the Food Pyramid

Look at the food pyramid. Which food group does each food belong to?

fish

bread

apple

cheese

ANSWERS: fish - meat and beans, bread - grains, apple - fruit, cheese - dairy